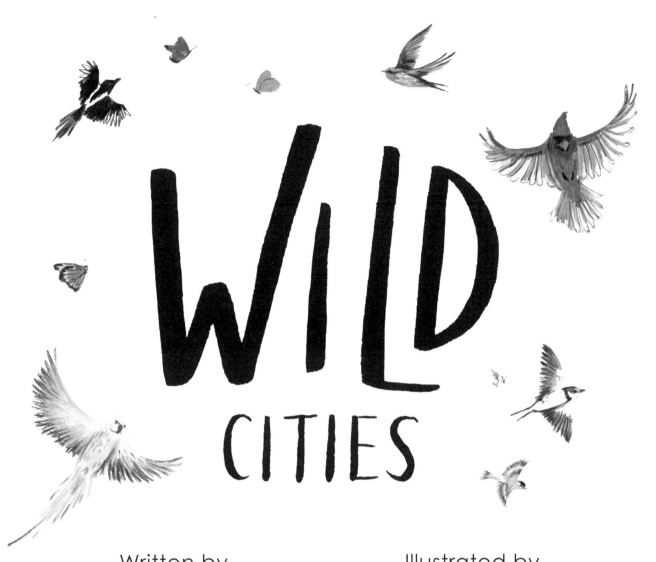

WILD
CITIES

Written by
BEN LERWILL

Illustrated by
HARRIET HOBDAY

PUFFIN

Our planet is blanketed in cities. Some are modern, others are old. Some are swelteringly hot, others are bitterly cold. Some have narrow lanes and chaotic markets, others have grand avenues and shiny skyscrapers. But one thing they have in common is that they're all crowded places – and they're getting even busier. Billions of humans around the world now live in cities, and this number grows larger every year.

But we're not the only creatures in this story. As our cities keep growing, more and more animals are having to make their homes in the city, too. For some, their habitats in the countryside are shrinking or disappearing. For others, the city is somewhere to stay safe from hunters and predators. And sometimes being around so many humans and buildings is their best way of finding shelter, warmth and food.

It means that today, perched on buildings, prowling down alleys and peeking out from trees, there are all sorts of city dwellers you might not expect to see. From wriggly reptiles to magnificent mammals, animals of all shapes and sizes are learning how to live alongside us. So look closer, and discover what can be found in our wild cities . . .

LONDON

is always on the move. If you could fly over the UK's capital city, you'd spot black taxis, bobbing boats and bright red buses. You'd see people hurrying past theatres, museums and royal palaces. The River Thames flows through the city's heart, while packed trains rattle through tunnels under the streets. More than eight million people live here, but they're not the only residents . . .

London was first built by the Romans almost 2,000 years ago and has been growing ever since, swallowing up areas of countryside. Some wild animals live here because London has grown so big that their homes are now part of the city.

Cities can sometimes provide what animals look for in nature: these bumblebees have learned to nest in hollow walls and gather pollen from city flowers.

In 1957, the River Thames was so dirty that experts called it 'biologically dead'. Now **harbour seals** are often seen near the giant office towers of Canary Wharf, catching fish and lying on riverbanks, while **dolphins** and **porpoises** are sometimes glimpsed swimming near the city centre, their dorsal fins gleaming above the surface.

London is well known for its quick and cunning foxes. **Urban foxes** were first spotted in the 1930s, and since then they've adapted to life here. They're clever enough to understand that crossing main roads is safer at night than during the day. Foxes feed on almost anything they can find: rubbish scraps, pigeons, insects, old vegetables – even meat bones or rotting cheese. They catch rats too, which helps keep London's rat population down.

Foxes can also be very adventurous – when London's tallest building, the Shard, was being built, workers found a fox living on the seventy-second floor!

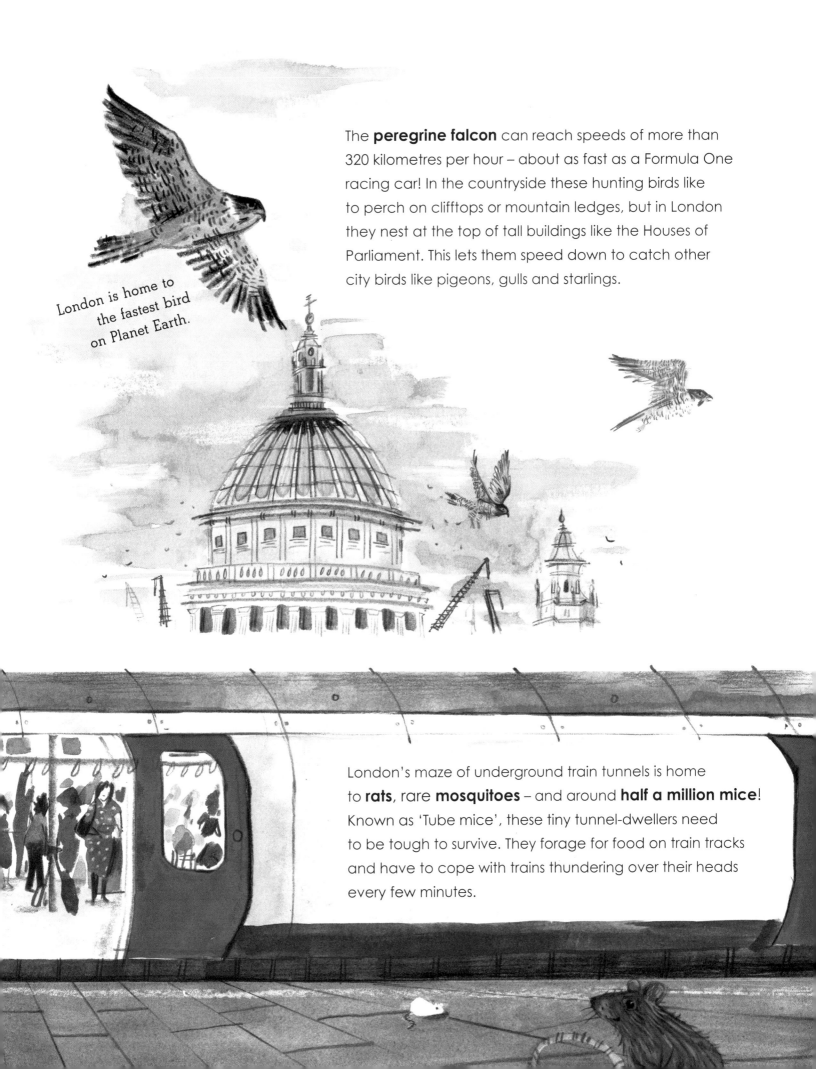

The **peregrine falcon** can reach speeds of more than 320 kilometres per hour – about as fast as a Formula One racing car! In the countryside these hunting birds like to perch on clifftops or mountain ledges, but in London they nest at the top of tall buildings like the Houses of Parliament. This lets them speed down to catch other city birds like pigeons, gulls and starlings.

London is home to the fastest bird on Planet Earth.

London's maze of underground train tunnels is home to **rats**, rare **mosquitoes** – and around **half a million mice**! Known as 'Tube mice', these tiny tunnel-dwellers need to be tough to survive. They forage for food on train tracks and have to cope with trains thundering over their heads every few minutes.

Richmond Park is usually full of cyclists and joggers, but when you look across its woods and grasslands, you might spot a pair of antlers, a tail, two big eyes . . . one of the hundreds of **red and fallow deer** that live here! In the seventeenth century, King Charles I of England built a brick wall around the park and brought in 2,000 deer to hunt. No one hunts here any more, and the deer can safely graze on grass and trees, chewing off all the low leaves and branches.

With their exotic green feathers and red beaks, these **parakeets** are more usually found in Africa and Asia – but there are thousands of them in London. No one knows who first brought them here, but nowadays the birds have adapted to the cold London weather.

A flash of bright green and a loud squawk – parakeets can often be seen in south London.

These impressive-looking beetles have become very rare in many places, but here in London they've found a home to thrive in. **Stag beetles** are happiest living in the dead wood of London's parks and gardens. They show us how important it is to let some of our green areas grow wild.

Stag beetles can grow bigger than an adult's thumb – but they're completely harmless to humans.

Tokyo

is the ultimate urban jungle: an all-action world of concrete, crowds and electric light. Or is it? Look closely and you'll find there's more to Japan's fast-moving capital than meets the eye. With endless hidden corners and a surprising amount of greenery, this isn't just a human city . . .

Perched on wires, roosting in parks or drying their wings near the city port, **great cormorants** are now a common sight in Tokyo. The water here is cleaner than it used to be, which suits the birds.

Fishermen don't like cormorants – they are too good at catching fish!

Jungle crows are experts at city living. They know which restaurants to wait outside for the tastiest rubbish, and how to distract pet dogs, then eat their food! In the nearby city of Sendai, crows have learned to drop nuts on the road as the traffic lights go green. The cars crack the shells for them, then the crows walk on to the pedestrian crossing and collect their nuts in safety!

Tokyo is full of hiding places, which is perfect for **masked palm civets**. They conceal their homes in temples, rooftops and empty houses.

These agile climbers can creep along balconies and power lines . . . often in search of food.

Once very rare in Tokyo, **kingfishers** can now be found sitting silently above ponds and streams, before rocketing into the water to catch a meal.

BERLIN

crackles with life. The capital of Germany is a big city with a big history. It has luxurious palaces, crowded squares and busy department stores. But it's also one of the greenest cities in Europe. Its parks, forests and marshes cover more than 30% of the city – and they're crawling with interesting wildlife . . .

The city has lots of 'green corridors', which link its wild spaces, creating a leafy road network through the city. These are perfect for animals to move around, and now Berlin has more fox dens in its built-up areas than in its forests. Sometimes these **urban foxes** can be very bold indeed – they've even been spotted riding the city's subway trains!

It might seem strange to us that wildlife would feel safer in a city than in the countryside, but this can sometimes be true. Animals are still hunted in some parts of the countryside, but here in the city this is much more unlikely.

The **goshawks** are the kings and queens of the Berlin skies.

Goshawks are silent killers, flying hard and fast at their prey. Berlin has more of these majestic birds than any other city in the world: there's so much here for them to hunt, and so many trees for them to perch in. They can catch city birds like pigeons and crows in mid-air! You might spot them at Tempelhofer Feld, an old Berlin airport which is now a park.

Not all Berlin's green spaces are sprawling parks. The city also has tens of thousands of allotment gardens, where people grow fruit and vegetables. These help to attract wildlife to the city too – although the garden owners might not always like it!

Several thousand snuffling, rough-haired **wild boars** live in the city, spending most of their time in the woods but often trotting on to the streets to seek out food. Berlin's main football team, Hertha BSC, has twice had its pitch destroyed by boars digging up the grass! Their sense of smell is three times as good as a dog's, which means they can sniff out a tasty snack from more than three kilometres away.

Some wild animals have lived near humans for hundreds of years, but for other species it's quite new. **Stone martens** are speedy creatures which usually live in mountains and woods. Because cities like Berlin have kept growing, they've had to adapt. Martens aren't always popular, because they use their sharp teeth to bite through the electric cables in cars. Why? The animals mark their territory by peeing, and if a marten smells a car that's been peed on by another marten, it attacks the car!

Stone martens find homes in house lofts, which are like the tree trunks and rock crevices they scurry into in the countryside.

These nimble whiskered **raccoons** are originally from North America – so why are there so many of them in Berlin? It used to be fashionable to wear raccoon fur coats, so German fur farmers started to buy raccoons. A few were released to be hunted – but then in 1945 a wartime bomb fell on one of the fur farms, and more raccoons escaped into the woods. Nowadays there are nearly a million in Germany. Raccoons can open rubbish bins and even turn doorknobs!

Raccoons get everywhere. One lived in the basement garage of a luxury hotel for a year and a half!

Between 1961 and 1989, Berlin was split in half. A tall wall separated East Berlin from West Berlin. The two sides had different governments, and people needed special permission to go from one to the other – but no one told Berlin's rabbits! Thousands of **wild rabbits** lived on the empty land next to the wall, burrowing underneath and making the most of being undisturbed. Today these wild rabbits have to make risky road crossings – but in some parts of Germany bridges have been built specially for wildlife.

SYDNEY

is Australia's oldest city, a place of blue skies, long beaches and deep harbours. Boats criss-cross the water, tourists take photos in the park and birds fly from tree to tree. In the middle of it all, the Opera House shines bright on the waterfront. Sydney is a wonderful city to live in . . . and animals of all shapes and sizes make their homes here too, tucked among the towers, hidden in the harbour and spread along the shoreline.

It's sometimes easy to forget that animals don't understand things like city boundaries. We might think that buildings, parks and roads 'belong' to humans, but animals just see them as different habitats they need to adapt to. Like us, they're doing their best to find a life that suits them.

Sydney Harbour isn't just beautiful to look at – it's also the largest natural harbour in the world. Some parts of it are 45 metres deep, which would cover the Opera House! Nearly 600 different species of fish have been spotted in the water.

Sharks can sometimes be seen here: the most common is the **bull shark**, which was gobbling up fish in the harbour long before the city was built. And if you look out to sea from Sydney's eastern beaches you might spot the giants of the ocean. Every year between May and August, thousands of **humpback whales** swim past the city, travelling up from Antarctica towards the tropical waters further north. **Bottlenose dolphins** can sometimes be seen too, darting through the waves.

Sydney's Opera House draws millions of visitors every year – including a **wild fur seal**, who has visited regularly since 2014, hauling himself out of the harbour to sunbathe on the steps near the water's edge.

The Opera House sits on a headland called Bennelong Point, so the blubbery visitor has been nicknamed 'Benny'!

When you think of Australian wildlife, one animal bounces to mind. With their enormous tails, large feet and long leaps, mobs of **eastern grey kangaroos** can often be spotted grazing in parks on the city outskirts. **Wallabies**, which are similar to kangaroos but smaller, can also be found in bushland near Sydney. Kangaroos and wallabies usually stay away from the busy parts of the city, but they can surprise us – in 2018, a male **swamp wallaby** was spotted hopping across Sydney Harbour Bridge!

Sydney's **powerful owls** are as strong and fearsome as they sound, racing through the night skies to feed.

In the countryside, owls fly for miles to look for food. But here in Sydney they stay within smaller pockets of the city, knowing they can find what they need close by. This is bad news for **possums**, because **powerful owls** need to eat the equivalent of one possum almost every night!

If you're in Sydney you're likely to spot the **brushtail possum**, a cat-sized creature with perky ears and super climbing skills. Much of its natural habitat has been destroyed to build houses and offices, so it has had to adapt to the city. Now it often makes its home in people's roofs and eats shrubs from their gardens. Some people love them, others don't! The city is also home to the **ringtail possum**, which can use its tail to curl around branches, and the **sugar glider**, a tiny tree-climber which uses flaps of skin between its front and back legs to glide more than 50 metres through the air!

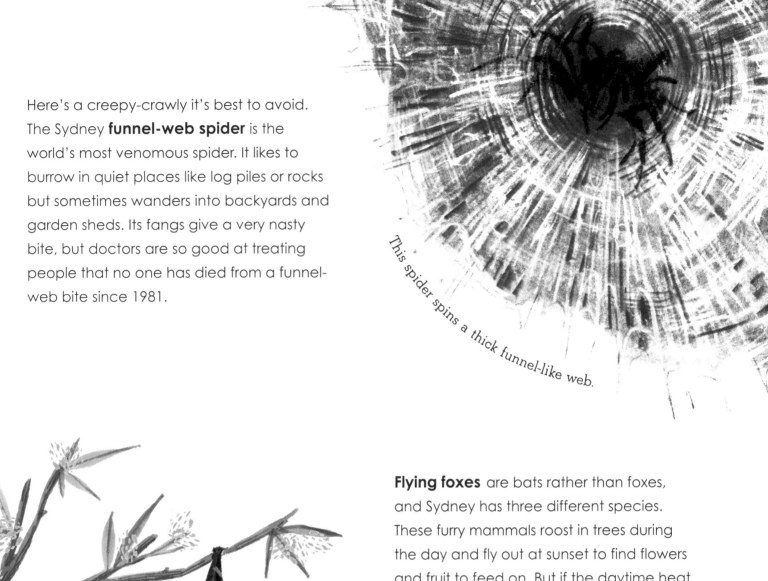

Here's a creepy-crawly it's best to avoid. The Sydney **funnel-web spider** is the world's most venomous spider. It likes to burrow in quiet places like log piles or rocks but sometimes wanders into backyards and garden sheds. Its fangs give a very nasty bite, but doctors are so good at treating people that no one has died from a funnel-web bite since 1981.

This spider spins a thick funnel-like web.

Flying foxes are bats rather than foxes, and Sydney has three different species. These furry mammals roost in trees during the day and fly out at sunset to find flowers and fruit to feed on. But if the daytime heat gets too fierce they have a clever method for cooling down: they swoop low over the city's waterways, dipping their bellies in the water, then lick the droplets from their fur.

WARSAW

covers a huge area and hides all sorts of fascinating sights and secrets. You could spend a long time wandering through Poland's capital city. In sunshine or snow, the wide Vistula River flows past hulking palaces, old libraries and buzzing backstreets. Poland is home to thousands of different creatures and many of them feel right at home in the greener, wilder parts of Warsaw.

Around 200 wild **red squirrels** live in Warsaw's Royal Łazienki Park. One of the reasons their numbers are high is because local people like feeding them, which means they don't often go hungry.

With the wilderness of Kampinos National Park so close by, forest animals sometimes appear in Warsaw. **Wild moose** occasionally find their way into the city's suburbs. Some even go swimming in the river! It seems these young males are forced out by their mothers when they need to find a new territory of their own. There's plenty of grass here for them to eat but the traffic and noise can panic a young moose, so specially trained rangers catch them and take them back to the woods.

Moose aren't the only visitors from the forest – people driving through the outskirts of the city sometimes spot **wolves** slinking past!

Poland has more than 100 mammal species, from tiny **field mice** to hefty **brown bears**. This impressive number reminds us that no matter where humans live around the world, and no matter how big our cities become, we're still just one mammal among many other animals.

Every summer, people sunbathe on beaches at the Vistula River . . . but not all of them know that there are other creatures in the neighbourhood. More than fifty **beavers** have been counted in the Warsaw area. These toothy animals are very clever, chewing off leaves, bark and twigs from willow and poplar trees, then keeping them in special underwater food stores.

Black storks are rare, and shy, but these birds are becoming less scared of humans.

Common tern

Human behaviour can be very damaging to animals – but we can help too. In 2011, Warsaw cleared the small islands in the middle of the Vistula River: perfect for **common terns** and **little terns** who make nests on the sand. These migratory birds try to stay away from buildings and humans, so being somewhere calm, in the middle of the river, suits them. Some of these pretty birds weigh less than a tennis ball but travel thousands of kilometres every year!

Imagine the tallest man in the world lying on the floor. A **white-tailed eagle** has a huge wingspan as wide as the height of that man! This giant bird of prey is a national symbol for Poland – Polish sports teams play with an eagle on their shirts. White-tailed eagles usually live in wild areas, but when forest lakes and smaller rivers freeze in winter they hunt for fish in Warsaw's Vistula River, where the waters take longer to freeze. Warsaw also attracts **ducks** and **black-headed gulls**, which the eagles like to eat.

A shape in the distance.

A half movement in the trees.

This is as close as you might get to spotting a **lynx** . . . but they are out there.

These gorgeous long-eared wildcats were once extinct in the countryside around Warsaw, but in the 1990s wildlife experts reintroduced them into Kampinos National Park. Since then the animals survive here in small numbers, eating foxes and rabbits, and jumping almost two metres into the air to catch birds! Kampinos National Park is a large nature reserve where city locals cycle and hike, but the lynx like to stay away from humans.

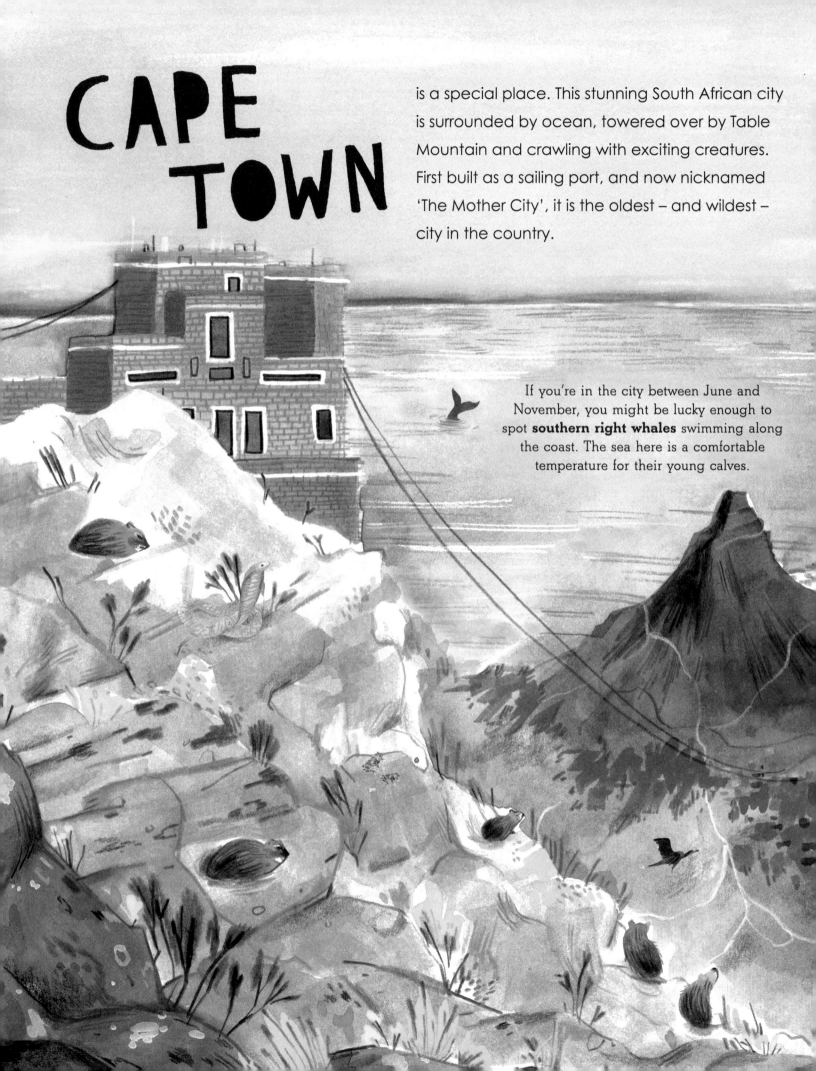

CAPE TOWN

is a special place. This stunning South African city is surrounded by ocean, towered over by Table Mountain and crawling with exciting creatures. First built as a sailing port, and now nicknamed 'The Mother City', it is the oldest – and wildest – city in the country.

If you're in the city between June and November, you might be lucky enough to spot **southern right whales** swimming along the coast. The sea here is a comfortable temperature for their young calves.

Found hiding on the slopes of Table Mountain, **rock hyraxes** are also known as 'dassies'. Incredibly, given how small and furry these creatures are, their closest living relative is the elephant!

Dassies like to forage for roots and plants on the mountain.

Surprisingly, these endangered **African penguins** have had
a colony here in Cape Town since the 1980s, living in the city's
sheltered bay. Local people help protect their nesting sites
and these penguins are now beloved residents. Sometimes
they have to climb steps and cross roads to get to the ocean,
where they can swim almost 100 kilometres on a single fishing trip!

More than **600 bird species** have been spotted in Cape Town, but none are so brightly feathered as the **orange-breasted sunbird**. They're often seen in the Kirstenbosch National Botanical Garden, where there are thousands of flowers filled with nectar.

When they're hungry – which is often! – **chacma baboons** are difficult to stop. They can climb into cars, steal shopping bags and even squeeze into houses. Several hundred baboons live in the Cape Town area and people are trying to learn how to live peacefully alongside them.

Often found lying lazily in the city's harbours, **Cape fur seals** are a common sight. Their wide eyes and soft coats make them look gentle, but their teeth are sharp. More than 60,000 seals live on Seal Island, a few kilometres out to sea. **Great white sharks** are often seen near the island, looking for a seal meal!

NEW YORK

is a city that surrounds you. Busy people and yellow taxis fill the avenues. Skyscrapers tower into the air. You hear the thump of music, the clatter of subway trains and the honk of car horns. You smell the sizzling scents of hot-dog carts. Life is everywhere you turn . . . but not all of it is human. Perched on buildings, prowling down alleys and peeping out from trees, the city's birds and animals mean this American metropolis has a wild side.

It seems impossible that you'd find 25-ton **humpback whales** just a short way from the bright lights of New York City, but it's true. The waters around the city, which used to be very polluted, are now cleaner, and these gentle giants are regularly seen swimming off the New York coast. They love feeding on silvery fish called **menhaden**, and new laws mean there are now more fish in the water.

When Central Park was first opened in 1858, lots of the park's trees and plants were brought in from other parts of the world – and so were some of the birds. One man released around 100 **European starlings** into the park in 1890s. Now 200 million of them live across North America – all descended from those first 100 birds! More than 200 **other bird species** can be spotted in the park, including **red-bellied woodpeckers**, **northern cardinals** and **red-winged blackbirds**.

Today New York is the largest city in the US. But a few hundred years ago, thick oak and chestnut forests covered nearly all of what is now New York. **Wolves**, **beavers** and **bears** used to live among the trees and streams.

Five different kinds of turtle live in Turtle Pond in Central Park. **Turtles** also live near New York's JFK International Airport, where they lay their eggs in the sandy soil. Sometimes flights have to be delayed because turtles are on the runway! It's possible that the Central Park turtles started out as pets released into the wild. This is a risky thing to do, because new species can cause problems for other animals.

Turtles aren't the only strange pets to have been released in New York – in 1935, the newspapers reported an **alligator** living in the sewers!

The heat of a busy city can help animals to survive. All the buildings, vehicles and people mean that cities are usually warmer than the countryside – and even a small rise in temperature can make a big difference during a chilly winter.

Birds of prey such as hawks usually nest at the top of tall trees, but some **red-tailed hawks** in New York have learned how to nest even higher. The best known was a male, nicknamed Pale Male, that built his nest on the side of a huge building on Fifth Avenue, twelve floors above the ground. When someone tried to remove his nest, people were very angry. The nest stayed where it was. Today red-tailed hawks can still be seen flying over New York, high in the air, looking for smaller birds and animals to eat.

They may look handsome with their smart stripes, but when **skunks** feel scared they squirt out a stinky liquid from under their tails. It makes such a pong that if it gets on to your clothes you might need to throw them away! Skunks were living in the New York area long before there were any skyscrapers, and these days they can find a good meal of fruit, eggs and small animals – all in the city.

New York's famous skyline helped to inspire the fictional Gotham City, where Batman lives, so it seems fitting that bats are found in many parts of the city. There are nine different species here, including the tiny **little brown bat** and the ginger-furred **eastern red bat**. Most of them only appear at night, when they eat lots of mosquitoes and other insects that humans try to avoid. Some bats can eat 500 mosquitoes in a single hour!

Around 8.5 million people live in New York, which sounds like a big number . . . until you learn that the city is also home to **1.6 billion pavement ants**! These tiny animals like living underneath paving stones, where it's warm enough for their eggs and larvae. They're experts at finding food dropped by humans, and they use their antennae to tell other ants.

SINGAPORE

is an island city that has attracted ships and travellers from all over the world for centuries. Today it's a modern Asian city with office towers, shopping malls and a fascinating jumble of beliefs and cultures . . . as well as some truly wonderful wildlife.

In the 1970s, **otters** had disappeared from Singapore, but the city is now home to around ten families of these playful, fish-catching mammals. Cleaner rivers and canals have helped bring them back. The otters have learned to be calm around humans and often cross busy parks, even sheltering under bridges and roads. The family groups here are larger than otter families in the countryside, which shows the city suits them.

Wow! This is the **oriental pied hornbill**, with its long tail feathers and curved, horn-topped beak. These large, eye-catching birds were once extinct in Singapore, so the city put up special nesting boxes. Now these hornbills are sometimes seen on people's balconies.

Singapore's first **Javan mynahs** were brought here as pets about 100 years ago – and now they're seen everywhere. The city once tried smearing spicy gel on tree branches to keep them away, but the clever birds just dropped leaves on top and stayed where they were. These noisy birds eat what they can – some even wait near busy road junctions for rubbish trucks to drive past!

Little egrets normally stay in green areas, but, as Singapore has expanded, these snow-white birds have realized that they can also find food in the shallow waters of the city's open drains.

Gentle and slow-moving with pretty, pinecone-patterned scales, **pangolins** are delightful animals. Here in Singapore they live in the forest, but they sometimes get lost and wander into buildings. Special wildlife officers help them find their way back.

PARIS

is a city where couples walk hand in hand, cars rumble down cobbled avenues and the smell of fresh bread drifts from bakeries. There's nowhere quite like it. The Eiffel Tower stands over the city like a giant and every year more people visit Paris than almost any other city in the world. But there's more to see in the French capital than the big tourist attractions. Look carefully – peer down at the riverbeds and up at the rooftops – to spot some fascinating urban wildlife.

Gaze up at the Parisian skies and you might catch sight of something special. **Kestrels** are fast, acrobatic falcons that have learned to make nests at the top of some of the city's tallest buildings and churches.

People think kestrels have lived in the city for more than 100 years, which shows us how well suited they are to city life.

Like so many cities around the world, Paris is packed with **pigeons.** The birds are everywhere – pecking, flapping, pooing and cooing – and people argue over what to do about them. Some people don't like them, because the birds can carry disease and damage buildings. Others think they have as much right to be here as humans. City pigeons are descended from wild rock pigeons, which live on mountains or clifftops, but here in Paris they perch on roofs, statues, walls and windows. Pigeons have done some amazing things for us over the years – during the First and Second World Wars some had to carry important messages, which they would fly long distances to deliver.

Paris is absolutely buzzing with **bees** – there are more than 1,000 beehives across the city. The bees seem happy here because there are plenty of flowers for them to visit and very few pesticides, which are chemicals sometimes used in the countryside. Some urban beekeepers say that bees produce more honey here than anywhere else.

Bees are tougher than they look. When there was a huge fire at Notre Dame Cathedral in 2019, the 180,000 bees living in hives on the roof survived!

Tall and noble with dagger-sharp beaks, **grey herons** are usually found in the countryside. But now they can be seen wading slowly and silently through city rivers and garden ponds. They have also been spotted in zoos, trying to pinch fish from the penguin enclosures.

With their serious-looking expressions, **coypus** look like they're always deep in thought. Maybe they're wondering how they ended up in Paris! These beaver-like river mammals are originally from South America but were brought over to Europe more than a century ago to be farmed for their fur. No one knows exactly what happened, but wild coypus are now found in many European cities. They've even been spotted nibbling on grass near the Eiffel Tower. In Paris there are few predators for them and they're also very good breeders.

Coypus can have as many as twelve babies at once.

A large **wels catfish** weighs about the same as two eight-year-old children!

When people first settled on the banks of the Seine more than 2,000 years ago, they would have found a river full of fish and other creatures. But as the city grew bigger and the water became dirtier, fewer species could survive. Today the Seine is cleaner again, and the river is now home to the **wels catfish**, a huge, flat-headed fish. It finds plenty of tasty crustaceans to eat and it grows quickly! Like all water-dwelling creatures, it can be harmed by rubbish that gets washed into the river, so looking after your litter is always important.

BEIJING

can feel like an enormous maze: children play in hidden courtyards, bicycles wobble down crowded lanes and buses zoom past towering temples. The city was made the capital of China 600 years ago and is now one of the biggest and busiest places on the planet. Everywhere you turn, there's something to see.

But wait! What's that fluttering over the road?

Is something scurrying along the wall?

And what's that tiptoeing through the shadows?

Beijing is an exciting place to be but sometimes the air becomes so polluted that people wear masks over their mouths and noses. It affects everything that lives here. The city is trying to help by creating urban parks and greenery.

What do you call a badger with a pig's nose? It sounds like a silly joke, but Beijing's **hog badgers** are very real . . . and very special. Slightly smaller than European badgers, they have big pink snouts. You might spot them in the wooded mountains on the city outskirts: life is still easiest for them away from humans so it's important their woods are protected.

Hedgehogs often need our care to survive.

Shh! What's that? It's the prickly pitter-patter of an **Amur hedgehog**, a shy mammal that nests and hibernates in the parks and gardens of central Beijing. City hedgehogs live slightly differently from countryside hedgehogs. They don't have so much space to search for food, and they're also far more likely to be disturbed by humans. The good news is that there are lots of things here for them to eat! If you live in a city that has hedgehogs, you can help by keeping some of your garden wild and making sure there are gaps in your fence for hedgehogs to come and go.

If you see a flash of yellow slinking down an alleyway, you might have caught sight of one of Beijing's **hutong weasels**. These slender golden-haired animals are mainly active at night. They like living in hutongs, which are narrow backstreets found all over the city. Life is better for them here than on noisy main roads. Spotting a hutong weasel needs luck and patience . . .

Hutong weasels are so quick, quiet and crafty that some people don't believe they exist!

In central Beijing, the Forbidden City is a huge palace where the emperors of China used to live. Beijing is now a very different city: between 1990 and 2010 alone, its population shot up from 6.8 million people to 16.4 million people! When cities grow at this speed, animals can lose their natural habitats.

Beijing is home to a few different wriggly reptiles.

You might spot a snake slithering swiftly under a hedge or a lizard dashing for cover in a courtyard.

You might even see the rare **Peking gecko**, which can use its sticky toes to scuttle up walls and across ceilings! Its mottled grey skin helps it to blend in against stones and walls.

Despite the air pollution, **500 bird species** have been spotted in Beijing – because the city is on one of Asia's main migration routes. This includes the looping, swooping **swifts** who visit only for a few months in spring and summer. Their other home is around 13,000 kilometres away, in southern Africa. Every year they soar halfway across the world without stopping – they eat, drink and even sleep while they're flying! When they reach Beijing, they hatch their eggs in the roofs of old palaces and other traditional buildings, as they have done for hundreds of years. Now, though, their numbers are dropping.

The locals are trying to help them by building special nesting boxes on high walls. **Swifts** help Beijing too, by catching millions of biting insects!

Some birds – like the **azure-winged magpie** – live here all the time. Often found in noisy groups, these graceful birds can feed on everything from seeds and insects to leftover rice.

CHICAGO

shimmers along the shores of Lake Michigan. The world's first skyscraper was built right here! Chicago is nicknamed the Windy City, but this US city is more than a metropolis – it's also a magnet for birds and animals.

More than 200 species of migrating birds pass through this area every year, including **palm warblers** and **indigo buntings**. But Chicago's famous skyscrapers can be dangerous for them. The birds get confused by the lights, so the city has a special team of people that cares for birds that have flown into towers during the night.

Big cats in Chicago? It's true! These hard-to-see **cougars** are sometimes spotted in the suburbs. On very rare occasions, they find their way closer to the city centre. Experts think the animals are trying to find a mate, or a habitat that suits them, and some become lost.

Ribbit! **Green frogs**, **boreal chorus frogs** and eleven other frog types are known to live in the Chicago region.

You can spot these good-looking **black-crowned night herons** in Lincoln Park Zoo – but they're wild. A colony of several hundred chooses to live wild at the zoo, making the most of the many trees.

Coyotes, which are mainly nocturnal, have learned to look both ways before crossing a road, and they've been seen padding through the heart of the city. In 2007, one coyote walked into a sandwich shop and lay down in the drinks cooler!

White-tailed deer often arrive on the edges of the city, where they find lawns to graze on. The animals will eat almost any plant they find, so they're not popular with gardeners. The city suburbs can seem safer from hunters and predators.

Green frogs

Cougar

Boreal chorus frog

Black-crowned night heron

Coyote

White-tailed deer

MUMBAI

is a tropical Indian mega-city bursting with sights, sounds and smells. Spices fill the air. Crowds throng the markets. Traffic clogs the roads. Over 21 million people live here and fill the hot, humid streets with noise, colour and activity. Food stalls sell fiery curries, washing dangles from balconies and three-wheeled taxis swarm across junctions. And, among all the hustle and bustle, there are eyes and ears in places you might not expect . . .

You're never far from the sea in Mumbai . . . and there are wonders to be found in the waves. **Humpback whales** and rare **humpback dolphins** can sometimes be spotted – and in 2018, for the first time in decades, **Olive Ridley turtles** came out of the sea to nest on Mumbai's Versova beach. These small turtles have heart-shaped shells and love warm water, but the beach used to be filthy, with plastic and rubbish everywhere. Then a group of volunteers spent two years cleaning it up . . . and the turtles came back!

Every year, tens of thousands of flamingos come to the city's Thane Creek.

The water here is full of the birds' favourite food, a blue-green algae which they hoover up with their big beaks. Funnily enough, it's a special pigment in this algae that turns their feathers pink! More **flamingos** arrived here in 2019 than ever before. Scientists think that sewage from the city might be causing more algae to appear in the water, which is why more of the birds are feeding here. This might seem like good news, but if the creek gets too smelly and dirty there could be no water left at all.

Monkeys are brilliant gymnasts, and in Indian cities like Jodhpur and Jaipur they climb railway poles, leap from rooftops and even snatch fruit from markets! Here in Mumbai their numbers aren't so high, but **macaque monkeys** can still be spotted swinging into the city looking for food.

India has many **urban monkeys** because so much of the animals' jungle habitat has been destroyed, so they have nowhere else to live.

In the last 40 years, Mumbai has lost around 60% of its greenery, so dozens of different snake species have moved into the city. **Snakes** are scared of humans, so most people here never see them, but some of Mumbai's snakes are poisonous. The city has a team of trained snake rescuers to safely move the animals to the countryside.

Twisting high through the sky, **black kites** have become a common sight over Mumbai. If a fire breaks out, kites often glide overhead, looking for reptiles and small mammals trying to escape the flames.

Despite their name, **black kites** are brown!

Look carefully as you walk through the city and you might spot a flitter-flutter of colour.

There are more than 150 butterfly species in Mumbai, including the beautiful **common Jezebels** and **striped tiger**. Butterflies stay in the greener parts of the city, which means they also show us where the air is cleanest.

Slowly, silently, the spotted cat stalks the city night.

Of all Mumbai's creatures, none are as awesome as the **leopard**. It might seem unbelievable but parts of Mumbai have more leopards per square kilometre than anywhere else in the world! They spend most of their time in the city's Sanjay Gandhi National Park, but at night they sometimes prowl into the suburbs, creeping past factories and apartment blocks in search of a filling meal.

The leopards have learned that people's rubbish attracts stray dogs and pigs . . . the perfect dinner for a hungry big cat. The outskirts of Mumbai have become hunting grounds for these leopards.

SEOUL

is a high-tech world of concrete, glass and steel. Power lines stretch between the buildings like spider threads, and the neon lights on the streets create a rainbow glow. Almost 10 million people live in the South Korean captial – but there's room for nature too.

Like many cities around the world, Seoul has tens of thousands of **homeless stray cats**. Most of them are descended from animals that were once pets. Their lives can be hard. Some local people leave out food and water to help them survive.

In 2005, a busy road above a city river was demolished to make Seoul greener. Now people come to the river to walk, paddle and relax. And just north of Seoul, South Korea is separated from North Korea by a strip of land where people aren't allowed. More than 5,000 plant and animal species have been spotted there!

Their name sounds like a funny insult – but these **brown-eared bulbuls** are well adapted to city life. Like many urban birds, they can open their beaks wide, which means there's more here that they can eat. The brown feathers beside their ears give them their name.

When **boars** don't find enough to eat in their forest habitats, some wander into Seoul to look for food. In 2017, two got lost and found themselves in a mobile-phone shop.

Summer in Seoul means the sound of **cicadas**. You might not see these winged insects – but you'll hear the male's high-pitched mating call. It sounds like an electric saw! Seoul's buildings make the city hotter, which the cicadas like. The city also makes the cicadas louder – because the noise echoes off the concrete and glass.

CALGARY

sits side by side with the wilderness. This proud Canadian city lies close to the Rocky Mountains, with lots of parkland and two winding rivers. Take a walk through its downtown streets, however, and you'll find a whirl of human life. People pour in and out of cafes and galleries. Noisy shops sell leather boots and cowboy hats. Tall office buildings loom over railway tracks and traffic lights. And this mix of the natural and the man-made attracts all sorts of curious creatures . . .

Calgary's Inglewood Bird Sanctuary is a special urban wildlife reserve. More than **270 bird species** have been spotted here, as well as **21 mammals** and **27 different types of butterfly**. Bring your binoculars!

Finding food in the city isn't easy for all animals. More than **10,000 mallards** shelter on Calgary's lakes in the winter, because the city's buildings and factories mean it's warmer here than in the countryside. But these handsome ducks have a problem. There's very little for them to eat in the snowy city, so they have to fly out across the fields to find enough grain to fill their bellies. When they're not hungry any more, they flap all the way back to Calgary to warm up. Some animals live outside the city and come in to find food – but these intelligent ducks do the opposite.

One summer's day in 2018, the middle of Calgary had a very unusual visitor. Walking among the road signs and street lights was something strange . . . **a moose on the loose!** These tall, long-legged creatures are the heaviest members of the deer family. Surprisingly, they seem unafraid of the city. Calgary has lots of green space and can feel safe for an animal like a moose, although local wildlife offices are trained to lead them back to the woods. They've also been spotted grazing near Calgary Airport and chomping apples in gardens!

The males grow big antlers each summer.

Porcupines are shy and like to stay away from busy places.

Is there something hiding under all those quills? There certainly is! **Porcupines** are tree-climbing mammals with beady eyes and thousands of sharp quills. They like Calgary's parks because there are plenty of green spots for them to shelter, and lots of bark and leaves to munch on. A local wildlife group in Calgary always asks people for their old Christmas trees, to give the city's porcupines a tasty meal!

These stealthy wildcats were once almost impossible to see . . . but the number of **bobcats** in North America has grown in recent years, partly because the winters are getting warmer. The animals are also learning to be less scared around humans. Some have been spotted swooshing through backyards and stalking along streets. Here in Calgary, they can find food, but sometimes attack family pets. With super-strong jaws, they can kill animals larger than themselves, often pouncing on their prey from above.

Fully grown **bobcats** are about twice the size of regular house cats.

Creeping through the suburbs comes Calgary's top predator.

Coyotes are quick-thinking killing machines with razor-sharp teeth and big appetites. Before the city was built, this area was their native habitat, but these clever animals have adapted well. They gulp down everything from rubbish to pet food . . . and sometimes even pets! Coyotes have always been a part of life in Canada, and the country's First Nations peoples have ancient myths and legends about the animal.

Despite their name, **white-tailed jackrabbits** are actually wild hares. Their grey fur turns white in winter, to help them blend in with the snow. Jackrabbits are most active at sunrise and sunset, but in Calgary some have learned that it's safer to move around in the middle of the day, when fewer predators are around and there's no rush-hour traffic.

Their top running speed is 55 kilometres per hour, which is much faster than any human.

One shaggy head. Four shaggy legs. A body as big as a barrel.

There's no mistaking a black bear – but you wouldn't expect to see one ambling past a shopping centre! Canada is famous for its **black bears**, which usually live in thick forests. Because they hibernate over winter, they spend autumn eating as much as they can to fatten up. Hungry bears have learned they can wander into the outskirts of Calgary to find fruit trees, berry bushes and rubbish bins. It's very important to keep away from them – these magnificent animals might be furry, but they can also be fierce.

All cities were built by, and for, people – but it's not easy to explain that to a wild boar or a baboon. Our land is also their land. No one can force a coyote to stay in the forest, no one can stop a bird of prey from flying where it wants to and no one can tell a fox not to walk down the street.

Wildlife and humans don't always live alongside each other in peace. But just like us, animals are doing their best to survive. As human cities keep growing, we need to find ways to safely make space for each other – so we can keep spotting majestic creatures, large and small, in our wild cities of the future.

There are all sorts of ways in which you can make your own difference, from little things like putting up nesting boxes and creating minibeast-friendly log piles, to bigger things like campaigning for green spaces and teaching others about wildlife. It's hugely important that we understand and respect the different animals that live alongside us – whether that's a mouse or a moose!

And the next time you're walking along a city street, make sure you look up, down and around. You never know what you might spot . . .

We spent some time looking for the wildlife in our own city, and it inspired us to create this book. Whether you live in a city or in the countryside, perhaps you can keep an eye out for your wild neighbours, and make them feel at home, too.

For my (sometimes wild) nieces, Sophie and Chloé – B.L.

For my parents, my biggest supporters and keen wildlife spotters – H.H.

PUFFIN BOOKS

UK | USA | Canada | Ireland | Australia | India | New Zealand | South Africa

Puffin Books is part of the Penguin Random House group of companies
whose addresses can be found at global.penguinrandomhouse.com.

www.penguin.co.uk   www.puffin.co.uk   www.ladybird.co.uk

 Penguin
Random House
UK

First published 2020
001

Text copyright © Ben Lerwill, 2020
Illustration copyright © Harriet Hobday, 2020
The moral right of the author and illustrator has been asserted

Printed in Latvia
A CIP catalogue record for this book is available from the British Library
ISBN: 978–0–241–43376–8

All correspondence to: Puffin Books, Penguin Random House Children's
One Embassy Gardens, 8 Viaduct Gardens
London SW11 7BW

 MIX
Paper from
responsible sources
FSC® C018179
www.fsc.org